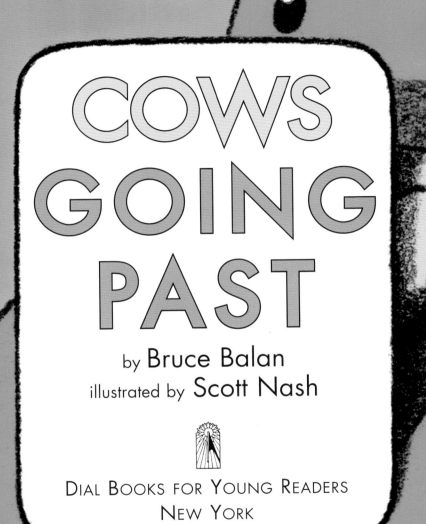

COWS
GOING
PAST

by Bruce Balan
illustrated by Scott Nash

DIAL BOOKS FOR YOUNG READERS
NEW YORK

For Dana
—B. B.

For Mike, Brenda, Elizabeth, and Kara. Welcome to Maine.
—S. N.

With thanks to Scott Whitehouse for his wonderful Photoshop design work.
—S. N.

DIAL BOOKS FOR YOUNG READERS
A division of Penguin Young Readers Group
Published by The Penguin Group
Penguin Group (USA) Inc., 375 Hudson Street, New York, NY 10014, U.S.A.
Penguin Group (Canada), 10 Alcorn Avenue, Toronto, Ontario, Canada M4V 3B2
(a division of Pearson Penguin Canada Inc.)
Penguin Books Ltd, 80 Strand, London WC2R 0RL, England
Penguin Ireland, 25 St. Stephen's Green, Dublin 2, Ireland (a division of Penguin Books Ltd)
Penguin Books India Pvt Ltd, 11 Community Centre, Panchsheel Park, New Delhi - 110 017, India
Penguin Group (NZ), Cnr Airborne and Rosedale Roads, Albany, Auckland, New Zealand
(a division of Pearson New Zealand Ltd)
Penguin Books (South Africa) (Pty) Ltd, 24 Sturdee Avenue, Rosebank, Johannesburg 2196, South Africa
Penguin Books Ltd, Registered Offices: 80 Strand, London WC2R 0RL, England
Text copyright © 2005 by Bruce Balan
Illustrations copyright © 2005 by Scott Nash
All rights reserved
Text set in Futura Book
Manufactured in China on acid-free paper

1 3 5 7 9 10 8 6 4 2

Library of Congress Cataloging-in-Publication Data
Balan, Bruce.
Cows going past / Bruce Balan ; illustrated by Scott Nash.
p. cm.
Summary: A family sees many different kinds of cows
from the window of their car while on a trip.
ISBN 0-8037-2902-2
[1. Cows—Fiction. 2. Automobile travel—Fiction. 3. Stories in rhyme.]
I. Nash, Scott, date, ill. II. Title.
PZ8.3.B179Co 2005
[E]—dc22
2004010826

The art was produced in black prismacolor pencil and Photoshop.

We are going.

We are going far.

We are going far

on a trip in a car.

From the window,

with nose against glass,

everything goes past.

Everything goes past . . . fast.

A town
goes past.

A tree
goes past.

A barn
goes past.

The sea
goes past.

But best of all, going past fast . . .

are cows.

A black cow

in a green field.

A white cow in a
brown field.

A red cow under a green
tree staring at a dog.

Bow-wow, cow!

A brown cow
and a white cow
asleep by a stream.

Do they dream?

Baby cows standing.
We wave.

A black-and-white cow
in daisies and clover.

White and green
and golden all over.

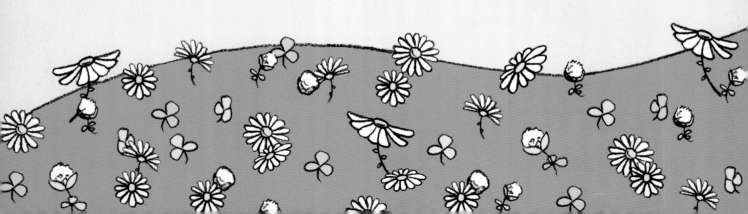

Spotted cows sleeping.

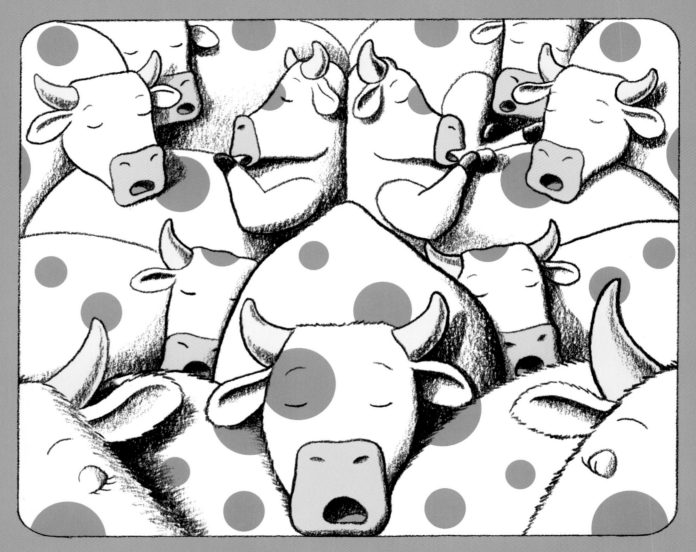

Shhh . . . don't speak.

Brown cow hiding.
Please don't peek.

Two yellow cows facing each other.

What do they say?
Hello or *Good day?*

One black cow,
all alone,
standing by
the blue sea.

Night comes.

Everything going past fast is black.

What was that?

Black cows in a black field
on a black night?

It's hard to tell.
There's no light.

The car has stopped.
Our trip is done.
We are finally here.
What was far is near.

Everything has gone past.
Everything has gone past, fast.

Good-bye,
town.

Good-bye,
tree.

Good-bye, barn.

Good-bye, sea.

And cows.

Black cows,

red cows,

white cows,

spotted cows.

All the cows
that went past. Good -

bye, cows.

Good-bye.